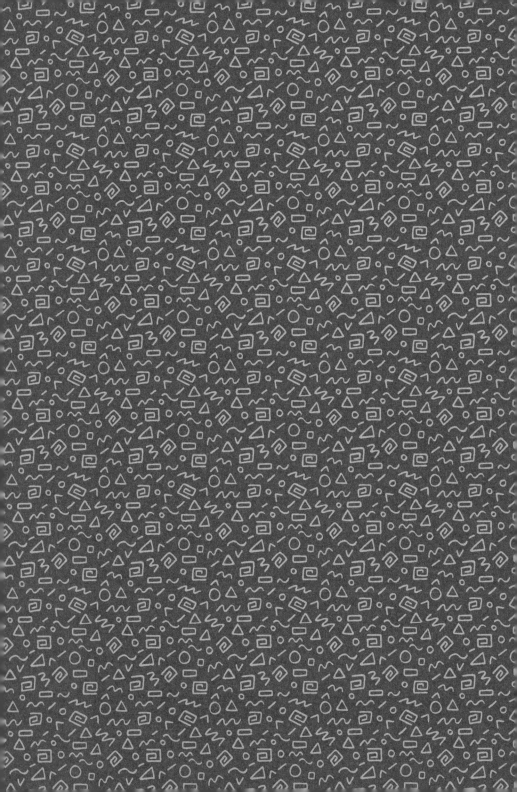

100% UNOFFICIAL

ULTIMATE GUIDE TO

STRANGER THINGS

DEAN

First published in Great Britain in 2020 by Dean,
an imprint of Egmont Books UK Ltd.
2 Minster Court, 10th floor, London, EC3R 7BB
www.egmontbooks.co.uk

Written by Amy Wills
Designed by Ian Pollard
Edited by Katrina Pallant
Cover designed by John Stuckey

This book is an original creation by Egmont Books UK Ltd

100% Unofficial Ultimate Guide to Stranger Things
copyright © Egmont Books UK Ltd 2020

ISBN 978 1 4052 9895 7

71106/001
Printed in Italy

Egmont takes its responsibility to the planet and its inhabitants very
seriously. We aim to use papers from well-managed forests run by
responsible suppliers.

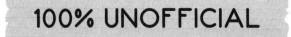

ULTIMATE GUIDE TO

STRANGER THINGS

All you need to know about
The Upside Down and beyond

Amy Wills

CONTENTS

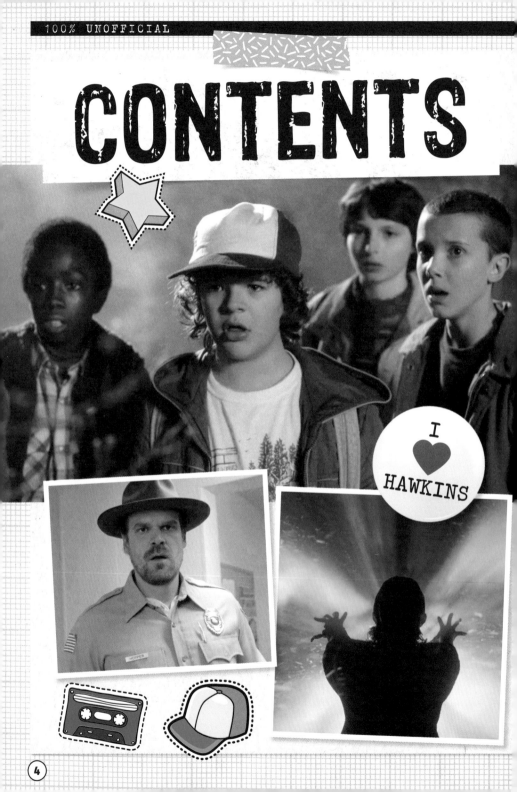

I ♥ HAWKINS

THE STORY OF STRANGER THINGS

How it went from word-of-mouth must-see to TV game changer.

"**W**hat if Steven Spielberg directed a Stephen King book?" That was how twin brothers Matt and Ross Duffer pitched *Stranger Things* to Netflix. When the first season landed on July 15 2016, with its retro black and red graphics and synthed-up theme music, few predicted it would become such a runaway sensation. In fact, over 15 other studios had already turned the idea down. But three seasons later, *Stranger Things* has become a cultural phenomenon, made stars of its child actors, won a load

of awards, spawned its own range of merch and made us all nostalgic for the 80s – even if we weren't even born then.

The Duffer brothers were though! They were born in 1984 and grew up in North Carolina. They became obsessed with Tim Burton's *Batman* and when their parents bought them a video camera, they started making their own movies. After film school they wrote and directed the movie *Hidden*, but it wasn't exactly a smash hit. They initially saw

The Duffer twins (actually wait they're just brothers)

The competition to see who was most excited got off to a good start.

Stranger Things as a film, but everybody they pitched it to said no. Thankfully, this was the start of the TV streaming boom, and eventually Netflix gave them the green light to make a horror/adventure show starring a bunch of pre-teen kids, a monster and some ominously-flickering Christmas lights.

The breakout success of *Stranger Things* has been attributed to nerd culture going mainstream (take the Marvel superhero movies), supernatural elements becoming cool (think of the dragons on *Game of Thrones*) and the hunger for nostalgia in increasingly challenging times. The internet went crazy for the

show's stars, snappy dialogue and cult references - leading to numerous memes and hashtags (e.g. #SAVEBARB). The third season was binge-watched by a record-breaking 40.7 million people around the world.

It's not clear if the fourth season of the show will be its last (after all, how many bad things can happen in Hawkins before everyone just moves?), but Netflix have signed the Duffer brothers up to make more TV shows and movies in the years to come, in a deal reportedly worth hundreds of millions of dollars. That's a lot of Eggos.

The third season was binge-watched by 40.7 million people.

STRANGER THINGS BY
NUMBERS

Beyond Eleven, obvs.

906
The number of boys they auditioned for the main roles.

 **1983**
The year *Stranger Things* starts. Hence the BMXs, VHS tapes, massive hair dos and high-waisted jeans.

 4.5
The number of hours it took the Duffer brothers to convince Winona Ryder to be in the show.

8
The number of a girl who was in the same experiment as 11. She's played by Danish actress Linnea Berthelsen.

20 hours, 50 minutes
The amount of time it would take you to binge-watch all 25 episodes.

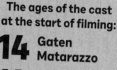 **The ages of the cast at the start of filming:**

14 Gaten Matarazzo
14 Caleb McLoughlan
13 Finn Wolfhard
12 Millie Bobbie Brown
11 Noah Schnapp

 28
The number of Eggo waffles Eleven eats. The number she pays for?

 0

 19
Romantic kisses (including Erica's dolls).

185

The total number of deaths in *Stranger Things*. Season Three was the most kill-heavy with 105 deaths. RIP!

336

The number of times people shout "Wiiiilllllll". Well, it got him back eventually ...

91

... of those were said by Will's mum alone.

32

Psychic nosebleeds experienced by Eleven.

20 minutes, 46 seconds

Total time spent in The Upside Down. And that's long enough, thanks. *Shudder*.

001-618-625-8313

Murray Bauman's number, as revealed in episode 6 of ST3. If you call it you get a secret message!

47

Pop culture references (although many superfans claim there are more).

1,200

Pounds of salt needed to make Eleven's sensory deprivation tank.

139

Number of times we see the Demogorgon.

18

The number of Emmys the show has been nominated for.

5

The number of Emmys the show has won.

6
NOVEMBER

Stranger Things Day – a holiday celebrating the show. It marks the date Will first went missing back in Season One.

*Number facts based on Seasons 1-3.

NOAH SCHNAPP

"I feel like I grew up in the 80s now from *Stranger Things*. But my parents always go, 'oh my God, I wore that shirt', or 'I did this'. So my parents relate to it."

GATEN MATARAZZO

"It feels like I'm playing myself sometimes. I don't want to play myself, I'm trying to be myself."

MILLIE BOBBY BROWN

"Everything you see on the show is what you get. We genuinely live in the 80s world when we're on set; everything, [down] to the underwear that we're given."

DON'T BE A STRANGER!

The cast on the strangeness of starring in *Stranger Things*.

SADIE SINK

"My friend had told me about *Stranger Things* and how I had to watch it. I was like, 'OK, I will!' I binged it in, like, a day and was like, 'Everyone needs to watch this.' A month later, I got the part."

CALEB McLAUGHLIN

"Being a celebrity, you know, it has its twists and turns. Not everything is good. Some things are great. But of course, there's pressure."

FINN WOLFHARD

"We shoot for so long on *Stranger Things* that I know Atlanta really well now."

SEASON 1

IT'S 1983

We go to Hawkins, Will goes missing, we meet Eleven, a Demogorgon is on the loose and ... Barb!

All important discussions happen at the back of the school bus.

SEASON 1 IN 30 SECONDS

★ There's shady business afoot at The Hawkins Lab ★ **Will Byers** disappears after a marathon D&D session ★ **Eleven** escapes from The Lab and meets **Mike** and the gang ★ **Barb** disappears and gets eaten by a monster in a dark scary version of Hawkins ★ **Hopper** finds out the body of **Will** isn't **Will** ★ **Eleven** enters the void to find **Will** and **Barb** (RIP) ★ **Eleven** destroys the Demogorgon but disappears in the process ★ **Hopper** and **Joyce** find **Will** and bring him home ★ Everything looks fine ... or is it?! *cue scary music*

STRANGEST THING!

The series was originally going to be called 'Montauk' and set in the Long Island village where they made the Spielberg film *Jaws*, but the Duffer brothers decided to change it to the fictional town of Hawkins, Indiana and film the show in Atlanta, Georgia, instead.

QUOTE
OF THE SEASON

"OH MY GOD OH MY GOD OH MY GOD OH MY GOD."

– Dustin, Chapter One

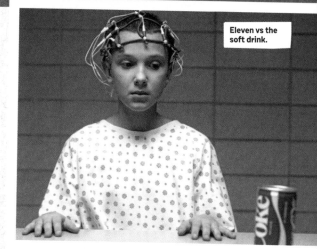

Eleven vs the soft drink.

Let's turn it up to Eleven

Eleven goes on quite a journey in Season One, from coke-can crushing lab rat to love-interest and hero. A key moment in her El-volution comes in chapter four, when the boys sneak El into school in a blonde wig, put her in one of Nancy's old dresses and Mike does her make-up. When she looks "pretty" he realises he might have a crush on her. Lucas isn't convinced she can be trusted and calls her powers into question ("She shut one door!") but by the end she's saving the day and giving Mike his first kiss.

Interior design goals

When Joyce Byers (Winona Ryder) figures out that she can communicate with her lost son Will through the lights in her home, she paints a Ouija board on the wall and hangs up Christmas lights so that he can send her messages. As you do. Everyone thinks the frazzled single mum has lost her mind, and when Will spells out R-U-N and the monster breaks though the wall, it's one of the season's scariest moments.

THE WISDOM OF
JONATHAN

"You shouldn't like things just because people tell you you're supposed to."

SEASON 1'S MOST MEMORABLE MOMENTS

Grab your christmas lights and stay away from The Gate, the first series of *Stranger Things* is an emotional rollercoaster.

SCARIEST MOMENT

There are a lot of jump-off-your-sofa scares in Season One, but perhaps the biggest shock comes before the opening credits have even rolled, when Will gets snatched up. Where's a fireball when you need one?

FUNNIEST MOMENT

Dustin gets some of the best lines in Season One, but when he gets on the school radio and adopts an Aussie accent and says "Do you eat kangaroos for breakfast?" a catchphrase was born.

SADDEST MOMENT

When we discover that gruff police chief Hopper's daughter, Sarah, died of cancer a few years before.

CUTEST MOMENT

After a hard day's monster hunting, Jonathan makes a bed on Nancy's floor, but she asks him to 'get up here'. He sweetly asks if he should leave the light on and they fall asleep together. Nothing like the end of the world to bring you together.

STRANGEST MOMENT

When Hopper cuts open Will's body in the morgue, and instead of innards there's just loads of cotton wool. What the ...?

MOST SATISFYING MOMENT

It's a toss up between when El beats the bullies ("Yeah that's right, she's our friend and she's crazy!") or when evil scientist (and El's 'Papa') Dr Brenner gets eaten by the Demogorgon. Good riddance!

What is *Dungeons and Dragons*?

The boys play a 10-hour session in the first episode, and it pops up throughout the season, but what is it? This fantasy role-player game first came out in 1974 and remains a best-seller. It involves a board, lots of dice (including one with 20 sides!), a player who acts as the 'Dungeon Master' and a monster called the Demogorgon. It's the ultimate past-time!

"MOUTH BREATHER!"

ELEVEN

Eleven and her telekinetic powers are the star of the show.

ELEVEN

The all you can eat burger contest wasn't going well.

Enter Eleven

When we first meet Eleven, she's escaped from Hawkins Lab and is sporting a hospital gown, bare feet and a shaved head. At Benny's Diner, she uses the power of her mind to fix a noisy fan in return for burgers, fries, ice-cream and a T-shirt. When Connie "from social services" turns up and shoots Benny dead, Eleven goes on the run again. Hooked.

Eleven to the rescue

The boys name her Eleven (because of the numbers tattooed on her arm) and she begins to help them find their missing friend Will. Eleven also lends a hand in other ways, too. When Mike stands up for himself against the school bullies, Eleven uses her powers to make the mean boy wet himself. When the same gang make Mike jump off a cliff, El swoops in and saves the day. She also flips a van to protect the boys. We all want an Eleven in our corner.

What the 'Ell?

In Season Two, when Eleven runs away to meet her 'sister' Kali, she gets a moody punk makeover, complete with eyeliner, slicked back hair and leather bracelets. Hopper calls it her "MTV punk look". Eleven calls it 'Bitchin'!'

Closing the gate

In the finale of Season Two, Eleven summons all of her psychic strength to trap the shadow monster and seal the edges of the gate together. Clearly it's her toughest feat to date as it leaves her bleeding from both nostrils at the same time. Do you want a tissue, El?

"The hurt is good"

OK, can we have that tissue back please? The closing moments of Season Three, when Eleven reads the letter from her (possibly dead) adoptive dad Hopper is a serious tear-jerker, and one of Eleven's most emotionally powerful moments.

MEET MBB

Born to British parents in Barcelona in 2004, **MILLIE BOBBIE BROWN** learned her American accent by watching the Disney Channel. She had cameo roles on shows like *Grey's Anatomy* and *Modern Family*, before four separate auditions won her the part of Eleven on *Stranger Things*. Alongside her acting chops, MBB has also displayed an impressive talent for singing and rapping. *Stranger Things: The Musical*? It could happen.

SPOT THE REFERENCES

Stranger Things wears its inspirations on its sleeve – these are just a few!

You wait ages for a bus and then one flips over your head.

E.T. PHONE THE DUFFER BROTHERS

There seems to be more references to Spielberg's 80s alien movie than anything else. For starters, the scene where Mike tries to hide Eleven in his room, is the same way Elliott tries to hide E.T. from his mum. There's also the scene where the boys try to disguise Eleven in a girly dress and a blonde wig, the same way Elliott tries to disguise E.T. And when the gang tries to outrun government agents while riding their bicycles, Eleven uses her powers to flip an oncoming van of government goons, allowing them to make their escape. Elliott and crew soar over a police blockade as E.T. levitates the gang to safety, in one of the most iconic moments in cinema history. No wonder The Duffer brothers told Millie Bobbie Brown to go watch the movie in preparation for her role.

Stand by all of us

The scenes where Mike, Eleven and co. trek along the old railway line harks back to the 1986 coming-of-age classic *Stand By Me*. The movie is based on a Stephen King short story 'The Body', which is the title of episode four of *Stranger Things* and is also about a group of friends who have to track down a missing boy.

Twin Peaks vs Hawkins

David Lynch's 90s TV show was set in a small town on the edge of a dense forest which hid a portal to a parallel dimension. Sound familiar? The *Stranger Things* logo and soundtrack are also similar to *Twin Peaks*. And when Mike looks at his reflection at the end of Season One, it's very similar to the final shot in *Twin Peaks* when Agent Cooper cracks his head into the bathroom mirror and laughs.

X–MEN MARKS THE SPOT

ULTRA NERDY!

In *Stranger Things*' first episode, Will wins a copy of a comic book: X-Men #134. The events and revelations of that particular issue foreshadow the plot of *Stranger Things*, as that issue of X-Men is the one where Jean Gray, the X-Men's powerful psychic, becomes Dark Phoenix, a cosmic being with dangerous and unstable psychic powers. Remind you of anyone?

THE FORCE IS STRONG WITH THIS ONE

There are plenty of *Star Wars* references in the show. Mike owns a Yoda action figure and is in awe of Eleven's 'Jedi powers'. When Lucas thinks Eleven is lying to the gang, he calls her 'Lando' - after Lando Calrissian, the character who betrays Han Solo in *The Empire Strikes Back*.

Don't look behind you, Nancy.

The *Alien* has landed

The slimy lifeforms that fill The Upside Down are a homage to the *Alien* universe. The most direct reference, however, comes in the final episode of the season. That's when Nancy sees Jonathan being pinned to the ground by the Demogorgon and shouts "Go to hell, you son of a b–!"- a reference to the classic scene in *Aliens* when Ripley, nuzzled in her power loader, fires off a similar order at the alien queen.

"IS THAT A NEW BRA?"

BARB—MANIA

How did Barb become the breakout star of Season One?

She's only in a few episodes before she gets sucked into The Upside Down after sulking by Steve's pool. And yet Nancy's best friend Barbara 'Barb' Holland, became an internet sensation. Fans were sharing 'Wanted' posters, memes, gifs and then 'JusticeForBarb' started trending on Twitter. Shannon Purser (who played Barb) was even nominated for an Emmy. So how did this bespectacled, straight-talking side-kick capture all our hearts?

Her fashion sense is on point

With her sweep of red hair, freckles, big glasses, high-waisted trousers and high-necked tops, Barb is a style icon.

She tells it like it is

Whether she's truth-talking Nancy ("He just wants to get in your pants!") or summing up a mood ("I'm chill") Barb gets the best lines. Shame there weren't more of them.

Everyone just forgot about her

When Will goes missing there's a search party, he's on the news and there's even a funeral. When Barb goes missing it's like "bye, Barb". What gives? She doesn't even get a funeral until Season Two.

Barb's pool party for one doesn't look that fun.

We want friends like Barb

She's the ultimate wingwoman, accompanying Nancy to Steve's party even when she doesn't want to go, spending hours picking out a top for Nancy to wear, and even joining in the fun just to be a good friend. What a hero.

In a world of Nancys, we're all Barbs

We've all felt like we're not the cool, good-looking, popular one in school. We've all studied for our chemistry test but still helped our friend who didn't bother revising. We've all felt ignored when we were getting brutally attacked by alien lifeforms ... No? Just Barb then.

MEET SHANNON

Barb was **SHANNON PURSER**'s first acting role (!) and she says she was "blown away by the reaction" she got. "Barb was written to be a throwaway character but really resonated with people. We all feel like the odd one out at some point." BARB FOR PRESIDENT.

"IF ANYONE ASKS WHERE I AM, I'VE LEFT THE COUNTRY."

MIKE WHEELER

The leader of the gang is the heart of the show.

MIKE

"My name's Mike, short for Michael"

When we first meet Mike Wheeler, he's leading the party in their D&D campaign in his basement, introducing his little plastic Demogorgon into the game. His face when his mum finds out they've been playing their campaign for ten hours is priceless.

This is basically Mike's bible.

Sharing's caring

Out of all the boys, Mike is the most sensitive. He's caring towards El, from their first meeting when he's hiding her in his basement and feeding her Eggos, to the third season where he's worried about what her powers will do to her. He jumps off a cliff to save Dustin, he never gives up on Will and he's also the first to realise Dart might be bad news. In Season Two, the tearful speech he gives about first meeting Will in the playground is heart melting.

Mike ♥ El

We all did a fist bump when Mike leans in to give El a kiss at the end of Season One. And when she finally walks into the dance in Season Two, it's all the feels.

"Muuuuum"

We love Mike's moods. From fights with his parents and his sister Nancy, to how grumpy he was at first to Max. He takes the gang's Halloween costume Ghostbusters so seriously, that he's angry when Lucas also turns up as Venkman. "We planned this months ago!"

Come on Mrs Wheeler, Mike's only been down there for 546 hours!

Sing it, Mike

Who could forget the opening of Season Three, when Mike is rocking out to some 80s power ballads? El would probably rather forget it, actually. She's not a fan.

MEET FINN

FINN WOLFHARD was born in 2002 in Canada. After winning the part of Mike through a video audition from his bedroom because he was ill, he's gone on to star in movies like *It* and *The Goldfinch*. Aside from acting, Finn is also a musician and plays guitar in his band 'The Aubreys'. Rock on!

He never gives up

Not only does he call El every day when they're apart, but he refuses to give up looking for Will. Mike is #friendship goals.

SECRETS FROM THE SET

A behind-the-scenes peek at how they made *Stranger Things* so strange.

Getting wiggy with it

Noah Schnapp wears hair extensions to play Will because his real hair is too short to get Will's bowl cut.

TANK GIRL

The crew really made a sensory deprivation tank out of a paddling pool. It took 1200 pounds of Epsom salts for Mille Bobbie Brown to float. She felt dizzy afterwards from all that salty floating around.

Monster man!

While Seasons Two and Three included plenty of special effects and CGI, the first season's Demogorgon was an actor. Mark Steger wore a monster suit and stilts with small amounts of green clothing so that his real arms could be made invisible on a green screen.

Kiss incoming

In the Season Two finale when Mike and Eleven kiss at the dance, Finn warned Millie that he was about to kiss her. "I swear he was like a ventriloquist," MBB said. "He goes 'OK, I'm coming in.'"

THE UPSIDE DOWN ISN'T SCARY

According to David Harbour, the actor who plays Hopper, The Upside Down isn't as spooky IRL. "For the spores, there's a dude with a big ol' pillowcase full of dandelions and a big fan. So you're walking down the hall and then this guy is just standing there blowing dandelions at you."

Make your own monster goo

Ever wondered what the slime Barb spits out in The Upside Down is made of? "It was a mixture of baby food, olive oil, some water, and some marmalade," says *ST* producer Shawn Levy. "It was some weird combo of ingredients, but completely non-toxic and, if necessary, edible. We did like 14 takes of that opening shot, and every time she was a gamer."

Caleb McLaughlin gives the set his thumbs up.

Cue music

Sometimes the directors play scary music during filming, to get the cast into the right mood.

IT TAKES TWO

Holly Wheeler (Mike and Nancy's little sister) is played by identical twins Anniston and Tinsley Price. You might also recognise them as Judith Grimes in *The Walking Dead*.

HAWKINS HOTSPOTS

The town might be fictional but you can visit some of the show's key locations in real life.

I ♥ HAWKINS

Hawkins Middle / High School

Much of the action in Season One and Two takes place in the corridors and classrooms of Hawkins school. Luckily The Patrick Henry High School, in Stockbridge, Georgia, which closed in 2015, could be used for these scenes.

The Wheeler's House

The site of Mike's many D&D campaigns, and where Eleven hid in the basement, is located at 2530 Piney Wood Lane, in East Point, Georgia, but don't go popping by for an Eggo!

The Quarry

It's where the police find Will's 'body' in Season One, and it's where bullies forced Mike to jump into the water before Eleven saved him. The real-life setting for these scenes is The Bellwood Quarry in Atlanta, which closed in 2007 and has since appeared in *The Hunger Games* and *The Walking Dead*.

Hawkins National Laboratory

The medical facility where experiments were done on Eleven, and she accidentally opened up the gate to The Upside Down. These lab scenes were filmed in the Georgia Mental Health Institute near Emory University in Atlanta, which closed in 1997.

Downtown Hawkins

This town centre was the place to be before Starcourt Mall came along. If you want to shop in Melvald's General Store where Joyce works, or the Radio Shack where Bob worked, you can head to 2nd Street in Jackson, Georgia where they filmed these scenes. Don't try the magnets, though.

Hawkins Police Station

Want to grab a doughnut with Hopper? 8485 Courthouse Square West, in Douglasville was used for external shots of the Hawkins Police Station.

Hawkins Community Pool

The pool where Billy and Heather work in Season Three is South Bend Pool in Atlanta. Just don't get locked in the sauna.

"I DON'T CARE IF ANYONE BELIEVES ME."

JOYCE BYERS

Will and Jonathan's mum was right all along.

JOYCE

Detective Joyce

Joyce is the first adult in Hawkins to believe – and investigate – what was really happening to Will. She's the first to jump into action in Season Two. And wait, why don't these magnets work? We all want Joyce to be on the case. Keep up, Hopper!

This is what phones used to look like.

Believe it or not, this is Joyce's happy face.

She's been through it all

She's rescued her son from an alternate universe after authorities tried to convince her he was dead. She's performed an exorcism on that same son. She's watched as her boyfriend was mauled by supernatural creatures so her family could escape unharmed. She watched as Hopper exploded as she closed the gate to The Upside Down. Oh, Joyce. You deserve a holiday.

Mother of the year

"This is not yours to fix alone. You act like you're all alone out there in the world, but you're not. You're not alone." When Joyce gives her eldest son Jonathan this speech in Season One, we see what a caring mum she is.

Christmas decorations are a bit odd in the Byers house.

She's determined

Everyone thinks she's crazy, but Joyce doesn't care. "Maybe I am a mess. Maybe I'm crazy, maybe I'm out of my mind! But God help me, I will keep these lights up until the day I die if I think there's a chance that Will's still out there!" Yeah, you tell 'em, Joyce!

Arts and crafts 101

Whether it's communicating through Christmas lights, or using all the paper in the house to get Will to make a map, Joyce is the art teacher we never knew we needed.

Who ya gonna call?

In Season Three, when Joyce and Hopper infiltrate the mayor's office, and his secretary picks up the phone, Joyce deftly rips the cord out of the wall, saying, "Who are you calling? The police?"

MEET WINONA

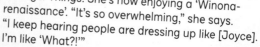

WINONA RYDER was one of the 80s and 90s biggest stars, appearing in cult movies *Beetlejuice*, *Heathers* and *Edward Scissorhands*, making her the perfect star to make a comeback in nostalgia-fest *Stranger Things*. She's now enjoying a 'Winona-renaissance'. "It's so overwhelming," she says. "I keep hearing people are dressing up like [Joyce]. I'm like 'What?!'"

SEASON 2

IT'S 1984

Life has returned to normal in Hawkins ... or has it?

Where's the Marshmallow Man?

SEASON 2 IN 30 SECONDS

★ **Joyce** is dating **Bob** and **Nancy** starts dating **Jonathan** ★ **Will's** visions of The Shadow Monster are getting worse ★ **Eleven** is living in a cabin with **Hopper** ★ A new girl called **Max** joins the gang ★ **Eleven** finds her mum and goes to Chicago to join her 'sister' Kali's gang ★ **Dustin** decides to keep a reptile as a pet ★ **Will's** map directs them to tunnels which are filled with Demodogs ★ **Mike** realises 'the Mind Flayer' is using **Will** to spy on them ★ The kids draw the Demogorgons away from **Eleven** as she closes the gate. Or does she?

STRANGEST THING!

Joyce's boyfriend Bob Newby became a fan favourite who saves the day, but gets eaten by a Demodog in the process. RIP Bob Newby: Superhero! Ross Duffer revealed that Bob was actually meant to die in episode four, and Will (possessed by the Mind Flayer) was going to murder him! Whoooooa.

QUOTE
OF THE SEASON

"HE LIKES IT COLD."

- Will, Chapter Four

With small pets comes big responsibility.

Steve: making sunglasses indoors a thing since 1984.

Dart attack

Dart – short for D'Artagnan – has a long journey from adorable tadpole to killer Demodog. Although he has no face or eyes, the special effects producers used his mouth to change him from cute to gah! "It doesn't look like the petal mouth of the Demogorgon," says Christina Graff, video effects supervisor on *Stranger Things*. So we went from the cute little tiny round mouth to the petal mouth, where it actually can open and you can see its teeth and that it's actually dangerous." Watch out Mews!

Steve's hair

Ever wondered how Steve maintained that glossy quiff of his? In Season Two we finally find out. "Use the shampoo and conditioner and when your hair's damp, not wet, okay? When it's damp, you do four puffs of the Farrah Fawcett spray." Sadly, Farah's hair products are no longer on the market.

THE WISDOM OF
MAX

"Hey guys, why are you headed *towards* the sound?"

SEASON 2'S MOST MEMORABLE MOMENTS

Dress up as a Ghostbuster, get your mind flayed and lock up your cat – the second series of *Stranger Things* ups the ante.

SCARIEST MOMENT

Either Will getting exorcised, or when a pack of Demodogs are chasing the gang through the fog and they have to hide in a school bus. *Shudder*.

MOST EMOTIONAL MOMENT

When Eleven comes back to Hawkins to save the day and is reunited with the boys in the penultimate episode. It's good to have the gang back together.

GROSSEST MOMENT

When Dustin's cute pet tadpole gets bigger and chocolate no longer satisfies his appetite. Dustin comes home to find Dart's tank is broken. And he's chewing on something. And where's Dustin's cat, Mews? Uh oh.

CUTEST MOMENT

The Snow Ball! Where Dustin coiffs his hair to look like Steve's and he gets to dance with Nancy. Lucas and Max get together. And Eleven and Mike have a proper kiss. Ahh young love!

STRANGEST MOMENT

When Eleven watches herself being born. After visiting her mother Terry, who is in an unresponsive state, Eleven uses her psychic abilities to delve into her mum's mind and watch her own birth. Creepy.

MOST SATISFYING MOMENT

When Max takes on her bully older step-brother Billy with Steve's baseball bat full of nails, shouting at him to leave her friends alone. Take that!

Video killed the radio star

When Joyce tries to watch Bob's video footage of Halloween to see who has been bullying Will, she tells Bob, "The tape ... it's shrunk". This is because most camcorders in the 80s used smaller VHS-C tapes, rather than chunky VHS videos. Which seems crazy when you think about how we can record on our phones now.

"MORNINGS ARE FOR COFFEE AND CONTEMPLATION."

JIM HOPPER

Hawkins' Chief of Police has been on quite the journey.

HOPPER

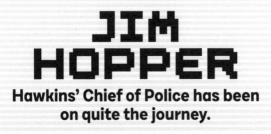

> We hope to one day be on the receiving end of *this* look.

Hopper 180

When we first meet Jim Hopper he's a chain-smoking drunk whose idea of police work is eating doughnuts and being sarcastic. But in fairness, the worst thing that's happened in Hawkins is an owl attacking Eleanor Gillespie's hair because it thought it was a nest. It's only when Will goes missing that Hopper overhauls his life, saves his town and starts living his best life. What a transformation.

Hop to the beat

While Eleven is living in the cabin, he tries to cheer her up by showing her how to dance to 70s rock star Jim Croce. Hopper's got the dad dancing down for sure.

Eleven took some convincing to leave the Eggos in the woods.

He's dad goals

OK, so he gets a bit shouty and overprotective in Season Three, but in Season Two when he's teaching Eleven about the word compromise (or COM-promise as he puts it) or when he's praising her for closing the gate ("You did good, kid") we see how caring he is. And don't get us started on the letter he writes her in Season Three. Weeps.

Be more Hopper

His answering machine message is "Hey, you've reached Jim. I'm probably doing something incredible right now." And given he's probably saving the world while wearing aviator shades, it's just a fact.

In Hop We Trust

There wasn't a more tear-jerking moment in *Stranger Things* than in Season Three, when Hopper gave the nod to Joyce to close the gate, sacrificing himself in the process. But is he really dead? Can it be? We Hop not.

MEET DAVID

DAVID HARBOUR began his acting career on Broadway and has spent two decades doing theatre, film and TV before playing Hopper. He's said that he didn't think *Stranger Things* would be a hit while they were filming it, let alone that Hopper would become so popular. But he relates most to the character of Mike in the show. "I was sort of the leader of my little band of nerds growing up."

SPOT THE REFERENCES

Let the wave of 80s nostalgia wash over you.

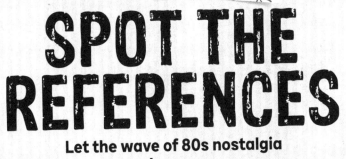

PAGE TURNER

In a quick flashback at the end of Season One, we saw Hopper reading *Anne of Green Gables* to his dying daughter. It's the same book he reads to Eleven in episode three of Season Two. It doesn't seem coincidental that the book tells the story of an orphaned girl who just happens to be ... wait for it ... 11 years old.

The doctor will see you now

When Eleven, Kali and her gang of friends go to find the man who helped Dr Brenner keep them captive, they catch him watching *Punky Brewster*. It's a show that just so happens to be about a young girl adopted by a grumpy old man, à la Eleven and Hopper. And the specific episode that he's watching? It's one in which Punky discusses having to go to the doctor. Very clever.

It's Mikey!

When casting Sean Astin to play Bob, the Duffer brothers knew a generation of 80s movies fans would remember him as Mikey from *The Goonies*. In the fifth episode, Astin even slips in a reference to his iconic role when he asks, "What's at the X? Pirate treasure?". Astin reportedly came up with the line himself.

Bob the brain is thinking hard.

STRANGER THINGS ITSELF

The show gets very meta when the writers make reference to the biggest criticism of their own show in episode five. When Lucas tells Max the entire arc of Season One, his new love interest doesn't believe him, claiming that the story was "a little derivative" and wishing that it were more "original." Good one, guys.

ULTRA NERDY!

TOP SCORE

The opening sequence of *Stranger Things 2* has the boys hitting the arcade. But did you notice that the game in which Dustin learns of a new challenger to his arcade prowess is called Dig Dug? No doubt it's a reference to how much of *Stranger Things 2* takes place underground, digging and dugging through the tunnels of The Upside Down.

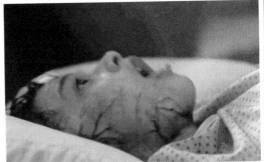

DIG DUG

BEST 5

	SCORE	NAME
1ST	751300	MADMAX
2ND	650990	DUSTIN
3RD	641183	LUCAS
4TH	620784	JKRACH
5TH	552415	

Be gone!

The possession of Will by the Mind Flayer recalls a number of horror classics, but *The Exorcist* comes most prominently to mind. It's especially pronounced in the final moments of the season, in which Joyce uses overwhelming heat to force the Mind Flayer out of her son's body.

"I COULD EAT A WHOLE BOWL OF NOUGAT."

DUSTIN HENDERSON

The smartest, funniest member of the gang.

DUSTIN

He's super smart

Although at first he seems like he'll just be the goofy, funny sidekick, Dustin quickly proves himself to be the smartest of the bunch. With his passion for science, he's the only one who knows how to use a compass. He identifies the shadow monster as the Mind Flayer and when he doesn't know the answer (Planck's constant, anyone?) he knows just who to call.

Dustin explains it all.

True bromance

When school bully 'King Steve' turns up with roses for Nancy, Dustin is quick to put him to work – telling him 'we've got bigger problems than your love life'. Soon the pair are inseparable, fighting monsters and swapping hair tips. In Season Three the bond is complete, with Dustin telling Steve 'If you die, I die'. Um, we just died ... of cuteness.

He brings the LOLs

Whether he's telling the school librarian 'these books are my paddles' or dressing in full hockey gear to trap the Demodog, Dustin is often the lisping, lovely light relief on the show. And we love him for it.

It doesn't look like we'd want to hang out there.

He's brave

Even though he was "on the bench" with Steve, Lucas and Max while the rest of the group went to fight the Mind Flayer and save Will, Dustin decided that he needed to go and help his friends. Against Steve's wishes, Dustin led everyone down into the tunnels of The Upside Down to get the Demodogs away from the lab in order to give Hopper and Eleven enough time to close the gate.

Best friends forever

Time and again, Dustin proves himself as a BFF. When the school bullies threaten to take out his teeth if Mike doesn't jump off a cliff into the lake he refuses to budge, and is willing to be tortured in order to save his friend Mike. He accepts Eleven (eventually) and is the one who brings Max into the group. Who wouldn't want to be friends with Dustin?

Let's hug it out, guys.

Sing it, Dusty-Bun!

In Season Three's final episode, Dustin finally gets his camp sweetheart Suzie on the radio. They sing a duet of *The Neverending Story*'s theme song and it's one of the best moments in the whole show.

MEET GATEN

GATEN MATARAZZO was born in 2002 in New Jersey with cleidocranial dysplasia (CCD), a condition which affects the development of bones and teeth. The Duffer brothers were so impressed by Gaten's audition that they gave the character of Dustin CCD. "When they wrote it into the show, I [started] getting a lot of messages and emails online from people who have the condition, saying that it really helps them come out of their shells a little bit," says Gaten.

STRANGER SNACKS

The show is a smorgasbord of 80s American junk food. A perfect menu for a ST party!

CAN WE GET **FRIES** WITH THAT?

DUSTIN'S DELICACIES

When Mike, Lucas, Dustin and Eleven head out to carry out 'Operation Mirkwood' to find Will, Dustin dumps out his haul of snacks, including Little Debbie Nutty Bars, Bazooka bubble gum, Pez, Smarties, Pringles, Nilla Wafers, an apple, a banana and some trail mix. "We need energy for our travels," says Dustin. "For stamina."

Snack Pack chocolate pudding

While they're hiding out at the school, Lucas and Dustin head to the cafeteria to find food. They come upon a stash of Hunt's Snack Pack chocolate pudding. "What's 'putting?'" Eleven asks Mike. "It's this chocolate goo you eat with a spoon," he says.

MRS BUTTERWORTH'S MAPLE SYRUP

This is a big hit in the Wheeler household – making its first appearance in the very first episode, when Nancy tells Mike he's disgusting for pouring it on his scrambled eggs. It's on the table again in episode six, when Karen makes the family pancakes.

KFC

The KFC family bucket became popular in 1969, and it's the focus of the Wheeler family dinner when Nancy brings her new boyfriend Steve over. When Nancy gets upset about Barb, Steve is left to awkwardly quote the 'finger-lickin' good' catchphrase. Awks.

Scoops Ahoy!

The ice-cream parlour where Steve works becomes key to breaking into the Russian lab (and has the best uniforms). Dustin, Robin and Steve offer Erica sundaes, milkshakes, and a Scoops Ahoy's USS Butterscotch ice cream boat to get her to sign up for their operation. She's willing to risk her life if it means free ice cream forever. It's a fair trade.

WHAT IS AN EGGO?

Eleven gets hooked on these frozen sweet waffles when Mike sneaks one down to the basement for her. Clearly she likes them, as when Eleven escapes from the lab she heads straight to a supermarket to steal as many boxes as she can, using her powers to slam the automatic glass doors shut.

After Eleven's disappearance, Hopper was able to find her again by leaving her boxes of Eggos in the woods. Hopper makes her a triple-decker Eggo extravaganza- an Eggo waffle sundae with layers of whipped cream, Hershey's Kisses, Reese's Pieces, and Mike and Ike candies. "It's only eight thousand calories" he tells her. Don't try this at home.

Eggos became popular in the US when Kelloggs bought the brand in 1968. Originally called Froffles (as in, Frozen Waffles), they now come in 10 different flavours and the brand saw a spike in sales thanks to *Stranger Things*.

SEASON 3

IT'S 1985

There's a new mall in town, rats are exploding and things just keep getting stranger.

Scoops Troop incoming!

SEASON 3 IN 30 SECONDS

★ Everyone loves Starcourt Mall (except the shops Downtown) ★ **Hopper** isn't happy about **Mike** and **Eleven** ★ **Billy** gets taken by the **Mind Flayer** and kidnaps **Heather** and her parents ★ Those rats are weird and **Joyce's** magnets aren't working ★ **Max** and **Eleven** go shopping ★ OMG there's a Russian Lab underneath the Mall ★ The **Mind Flayer** creates a fleshy army of possessed people ★ **Joyce** and **Hopper** kidnap Russian scientist **Alexei** and take him to **Murray** ★ **Billy** sacrifices himself to save **Eleven** ★ **Hopper** sacrifices himself to save everyone ★ The **Byers** and **Eleven** leave Hawkins, bye!

STRANGEST * THING!

Those exploding rats took some time to get right. Visual effects supervisors studied real rats, then made CGI and puppet rats to get the final look. And the gooey monster made of people? It was supposed to look like Play-Doh made up of bones and tissues. Gross!

QUOTE
OF THE SEASON
"YOU CAN'T SPELL AMERICA WITHOUT ERICA."

– Erica, Chapter Four

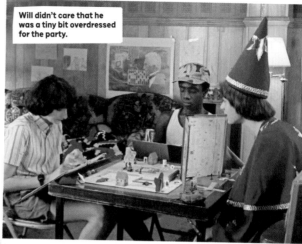

Will didn't care that he was a tiny bit overdressed for the party.

Will's breakdown

Will The Wise wants to get stuck into a few D&D campaigns, but Lucas and Mike are having girl trouble. Cut to Will destroying 'Castle Byers' in the rain. One of the saddest moments in what turns out to be a very sad series.

Hold on a minute...

Just when you think Season Three is over, Hopper is dead and the credits have rolled, we cut to a Russian prison, where a guard is told "not the American" before he feeds another prisoner to a captive Demogorgon. Is 'the American' Hopper?! The teaser trailer for Season Four suggests we might be right ...

Steve wins a fight! (His first!)

Some big things are happening in Season Three – there's a giant flesh monster made of townspeople and Mike admits he loves Eleven. But let's take a moment to appreciate the fact that Steve wins his first ever fight. Against a Russian in the lab. Kapow!

THE WISDOM OF
MAX

"There's more to life than stupid boys you know."

SEASON 3'S MOST MEMORABLE MOMENTS

Snacking on fertiliser, building a giant flesh monster and hanging out at the mall. Let's kick it!

GIRL POWER MOMENT

While her misogynistic bosses were belittling "Nancy Drew" and ignoring the story, Nancy Wheeler was determined to stay on the case of the diseased rats. Thankfully her mother was on hand with a pep talk. It's touching and powerful. You go Wheeler women!

SCARIEST MOMENT

When the Mind Flayed Bruce and Tom are chasing Nancy and Jonathan through the hospital, with flickering lights and swooshed back curtains. Rusty scissors? Creepy-sounding "Marco Polo"? This had all the staples of a horror movie special.

GROSSEST MOMENT

The image of sweet old lady Mrs Driscoll looking up at Steve and Nancy while chomping down on a bag of fertiliser in her basement is seared into our brains forever.

CUTEST MOMENT

Maya Hawke's Robin was the breakout star of Season Three. Robin coming out to Steve after they escape Russian soldiers made our hearts melt quicker than a Scoops Ahoy sundae. And then they went back to puking up and laughing and saving the world.

STRANGEST MOMENT

When the kids decide to lock Billy in the sauna to test if he's one of the flayed, we suddenly feel sympathy for him, as he battles the monster that's taken over his mind and body. "Please believe me. I tried to stop him," he tearfully pleads with his stepsister, Max. Poor Billy.

MOST SHOCKING MOMENT

We'd just started to warm to Alexei, and he was having all the fun of the fair – winning toys and about to taste his first corn dog – when the Russian muscly dude in a vest comes out of nowhere and shoots him. Look out!

What is Planck's Constant?

In the final episode the fate of the entire world rests on Suzie's ability to remember Planck's Constant and unlock the door to the underground lab. So what is this magic number? Named for the German physicist Max Planck, Planck's constant describes the behaviour of particles and waves, including the particle of light, the photon. Planck's constant is represented by h, and is: $6.62607015 \times 10^{-34}$ Joule-seconds. Super-super-super nerdy x 10!

"FIRST OF ALL, IT'S A WRIST-ROCKET ..."

LUCAS SINCLAIR

He's the bandana-wearing voice of reason and a master with a slingshot.

LUCAS

Who ya gonna call? LUCAS!

The master of suspicious face

While everyone else is freaking out about aliens and The Upside Down, Lucas Sinclair is the discerning, sceptical member of the group. He questions everything. Including Eleven. He ain't buying anything until he sees the proof, and for that, we love him.

Nice shot!

Lucas is a master of his Wrist Rocket and uses it to shoot the Demogorgon. When they trap Billy in the sauna in Season Three, he uses his slingshot to knock him out. He also shoots a balloon at the Mind Flayer to save his friends from getting eaten. We'd want Lucas on our team.

Lucas = the best at giving backies.

Lucas the charmer

No wonder the bad-ass new girl in Hawkins, aka Max, falls for Lucas. Although Dustin also liked her (and went to Steve for advice on how to woo her), Lucas made her feel part of the gang and for that he got rewarded with a kiss at The Snow Ball. Their relationship develops and matures in Season Three, so that Lucas is able to give dating advice to Mike.

Lucas to the rescue!

He comes "hella prepared" and shows no fear in the face of the Mind Flayer – cutting off its tentacle with an axe to save Eleven. He also comes up with the idea to use fireworks to tackle it. Good thinking, Lucas!

It's Lucas's turn next, OK Dustin?

Style icon

The camo bandana, the vest top, the sweatbands and the shearling jacket. Lucas has got a strong style game. All accessorised with a slingshot.

MEET CALEB

CALEB MCLOUGHLIN was born in 2001 in a small town in New York State and like Gaten (Dustin) appeared on Broadway before winning the part in *Stranger Things*. And Lucas' iconic bandana was his idea! "I felt like Lucas would want a bandana because he was into combat and the army. So I just asked, 'Can I get a bandana over here?' I had the privilege to do that," he says.

SPOT THE REFERENCES

SEASON 3

How many of these did you pick up on?
Free Scoops Ahoy if you got more than three.

HOPPER, PI

Magnum, PI was a hit TV show in the 80s starring Tom Selleck as a private detective who solves crimes in Hawaii while wearing colourful tropical shirts, sporting an impressive moustache and driving a sports car. We think Hopper might have been a fan.

Who's he?

Best known, then and now, as the star of 1984's *The Karate Kid*, Ralph Macchio was a teen magazine staple in the 1980s. Despite his youthful appearance, Macchio was already 21 when he first played the aspiring karate star Daniel LaRusso, a role he reprised in two sequels. With its story of a transplant to a new culture learning to make his way in a strange, hostile world, *The Karate Kid* would probably appeal to El.

Material Girls

El and Max go shopping to Madonna's era-defining *Material Girl*, the second single from Madonna's hit 1984 album *Like a Virgin*. Perfection.

DEAD RINGER

The Hawkins blackout occurs as Mike, Will, Lucas and Max are watching the zombie movie *Day of the Dead*. A later scene in the episode will provide another nod to Romero, shooting Hawkins's neglected downtown in much the way *Day of the Dead* depicts the abandoned Florida city seen early in the film.

Fast Times at Starcourt

Starcourt Mall resembles Ridgemont Mall from the movie *Fast Times at Ridgemont High*. Plus, the humiliating sailor costume Steve wears as his Scoops Ahoy uniform, is a direct homage to the pirate costume worn by Judge Reinhold's *Fast Times* character while working at Captain Hook Fish & Chips. Ahoy there!

THE MIND FLAYER

The Mind Flayer is much more evolved than the Demodogs, controlling both them and poor Will. It's described as a virus, even infecting Hawkins itself thanks to the elaborate system of tunnels it builds under the town.

Demo-people?

In Season Three the Mind Flayer returns to terrorise Hawkins, and this time the gooey baddie controls people and, er, rats. It then assembles them, liquidises them and turns them into one big sticky scary monster.

IS IT OVER NOW?

Destroying the machine in the Russian facility closed the gate to The Upside Down once and for all, severing the Mind Flayer from our world and killing its monstrous weapon in the process. We know this because the finale didn't hop to some looming image of the Mind Flayer over Hawkins like last season. Instead, *Stranger Things* signals it has moved on to another villain by showing a Demogorgon being kept alive in a Russian prison. What does this mean? Only Season Four will reveal the answers.

We get why Mike might have a fear of spiders.

THE UPSIDE DOWN

Here's everything we know about the alternate dimension.

The Vale of Shadow

The boys use words from *Dungeons and Dragons* to explain things in The Upside Down. They name the creature stalking Hawkins the "Demogorgon" after a monster in the game. Dustin compares The Upside Down to the "Vale of Shadows."

Eleven and the substitute teacher weren't getting on well.

Eleven started it

After encountering a monster while using her psychokinesis in a sensory-deprivation tank in Hawkins Lab, Eleven freaks out and tears the fabric between our world and The Upside Down, unleashing a whole lot of trouble known as Season One of *Stranger Things*. But is The Upside Down part of a multiverse, one of an infinite number of other worlds?

DEMODOGS?

In Season Two we learn that the Demogorgon has relatives! Dustin names them "Demodogs" because, well, they are the size of giant dogs and run around in bloodthirsty packs. But these Demodogs are merely minions of Season Two's true big baddie, the Mind Flayer, also known as the Shadow Monster.

"ASK FOR FORGIVENESS, NOT PERMISSION."

NANCY WHEELER

From preppy schoolgirl sweetheart to Demogorgon-shooting badass.

NANCY

What a journey

Nancy goes from self-absorbed teenager who only cares about kissing Steve (What about Barb, eh?), to a queen of truth and justice. And that's just in the first season. Wow. Her transition from the girl next door to the Hawkins hero is truly remarkable.

Nancy wonders if there might be a better boyfriend nearby.

She's brave

Despite having gone to the creepy blue-tinted Upside Down in that tree, and knowing that it stole her best friend, Nancy still chooses to go back there and fight the Demogorgon. When Hopper asks who knows how to use a gun, Nancy is the first to pipe up. Fierce, girl!

The couple that saves Hawkins together, stays together.

Nancy loves ...?

The love triangle storyline still has fans divided over whether she should've ended up with bad boy Steve Harrington or sweet and sensitive Jonathan. But since the first moment we see Nancy and Jonathan on screen, it's clear how strong their feelings are. And these two have weathered a lot – missing brothers, getting sacked from the newspaper and, er, Murray's pull-out bed.

She's sweet

Although she's previously rebuffed her little brother's mate Dustin and his offer of pizza by shutting a door in his face, she later cheers him up by dancing with him at the ball, telling him "You know, out of all of my brother's friends, you're my favourite. You've always been my favourite." Nancy, you're our favourite.

Truth teller

Nancy avenges Barb's death and gets the Hawkins Lab shut down. She's the only one who pursues the weird rats and fertiliser story, even though no one at her newspaper believes her. Everyone should just listen to Nancy, OK?

MEET NATALIA

NATALIA DYER was born in 1995 in Nashville, Tennessee and got her first big role in *Hannah Montana: The Movie*. But when she landed the part of Nancy on *Stranger Things* not only did it catapult her to fame, it also found her love – as Natalia and Charlie Heaton (who plays Jonathan) are a couple IRL! "It's an interesting thing to work with somebody who you go home with," says Natalia. "It's always really fun [...] We're really comfortable with each other."

QUESTION TIME

Season Three is over, but we still have some lingering questions ...

WE NEED ANSWERS!

Who is The American?

At the end of Season Three we're in a Russian prison, and the guards are told to feed a prisoner to the Demogorgon, but not "The American". Is it Hopper? We never saw his body after all. Is it Dr Brenner – the lab scientist who we were told is still alive in Season Two? Is it Barb?! And why is there a Demogorgon in Russia anyway? Is this scene even set in the present, or is it going back in time? SO. MANY. QUESTIONS.

Will Eleven get her powers back?

Eleven can't crush a coke can or even get down a teddy from the top of the wardrobe at the end of Season Three. Mike is confident she'll get her powers back, but when? And how will she save the world without them?

Is the Mind Flayer gone?

The Mind Flayer's body is dead by Season Three's end, but is its consciousness still alive and kicking? When Eleven closed the gate on the Mind Flayer in the Season Two finale the Mind Flayer left a souvenir in Will, so who knows, maybe!

Will Season Four be in Hawkins?

Given that so much bad stuff has happened in one small town, we wouldn't be surprised if the next season is set somewhere else. Will it be the un-named town where the Byers and Eleven are moving to? Will it be a completely new city with a new cast?

Will we see more Suzie?

Although Dustin was mocked for having an imaginary girlfriend from camp, we finally get to see Suzie in the last episode when she remembers Planck's Constant and sings *The Neverending Story* with 'Dusty Bun'. Will Season Four develop this relationship? We hope so.

Um, where are their parents?

Other than Joyce, no one's parents really seem to care where the kids are. And who is going to take care of Max now that Billy is dead? Hopefully not that creepy stepdad.

HAUTE HAWKINS

Stranger Things is a seriously stylish show, but here are the top fashion moments.

Bitchin'

Eleven spends most of Season Two in a dowdy plaid shirt in Hopper's cabin, so when she gets her punk makeover in Kali's gang, it's a big moment. That is some serious eyeliner.

Barb (of course)

One of the key reasons Barb was such a popular character was her incredibly on-trend look. Oversized glasses, high-waisted jeans, ruffle shirts. Barb, we salute you.

Double denim

Billy's 'bad boy' denim jacket and jeans look is pure 80s Americana. Shirt unbuttoned to the naval is actually pretty covered up for Billy, considering he spends 90% of the show topless.

ZIP IT UP

Steve's friends Vicki, Tina and Carol may not have the biggest parts on the show, but their 80s bomber jackets are never to be forgotten.

Date night

When Hopper changes out of his sheriff's uniform to take Joyce for a date, he looks seriously dapper in a white suit and a Hawaiian shirt. Sadly she's too freaked out by her magnets to show up.

Steve 'the hair' Harrington

But it's not just about the hair. The Ray-Ban sunglasses, the Members Only grey jacket and super tight jeans make him the ultimate 80s hunk.

In there like swimwear

Karen Wheeler really brings her fashion A-game to the pool (nothing to do with Billy being the lifeguard obviously). Her two-tone swimsuit (with full make-up) is a look we all want.

MAX-EL

When Max takes Eleven to the mall to go shopping it's one of the show's strongest fashion episodes, with the girls rocking several fresh looks – think bold, 80s print shirts and scrunchies. Epic.

"BEING A FREAK IS THE BEST."

JONATHAN BYERS

The softly-spoken sensitive snapper and Will's big brother.

JONATHAN

Jonathan and Will catching up about music, and y'know, monsters.

He's the best big brother

Jonathan has some great bonding moments with Will, from making him mixtapes of The Clash to telling him not to worry about being normal. "Who would you rather be friends with? Bowie or Kenny Rogers?" Fair point, Jonathan.

Artist in residence

Jonathan is that guy everyone knows who's super into photography. Never without his camera, he says things like "Sometimes people don't really say what they're really thinking. But when you capture the right moment, it says more."

He's sensitive ...

The eldest Byers son is always tuned in to other people's distress and is very sweet and caring. When his dad shot a rabbit, he cried for nine days. Poor Jonathan!

It's good to talk (and cry).

... but don't mess with him

Although he seems quiet, when it comes down to it Jonathan is tough. Like when Steve breaks his camera ... and so Jonathan breaks his face. Sorry Steve but you had it coming.

Wrong move

Jonathan often gets it right, but if he doesn't he admits it. "I was completely awfully mortifyingly wrong," he tells Nancy in Season Three. And then he saves her from the monster. Swoon.

MEET CHARLIE

CHARLIE HEATON was born in Leeds in 1994 and was a drummer in the rock band Comanechi before getting the part of Jonathan. "I don't think anyone could predict how popular *Stranger Things* was going to get," he says. "I remember when we were filming Season One, wondering if anyone was going to watch this show". Next up he's starring in *X-Men* spin-off *New Mutants*.

STRANGER DANGER!

The scariest ever moments on *Stranger Things*.

WHERE'S WILL?

When the monster chases Will home and he hides in the shed, it's pretty edge-of-the-sofa stuff. But when the light goes off, and Will has disappeared it gives us that chilly cold neck thing which Will gets the whole time. The show hasn't even started yet and we're already scared!

MONSTER MASH

The scenes where Nancy, Steve and Jonathan battle the monster with rocks, bats, a lighter and everything they can lay their hands on are some of the jumpiest moments in Season One.

TOILET BREAK

Will excuses himself to go to the bathroom, only to cough up a black slug-like creature into the sink. The Upside Down isn't far away after all. *Shudder*.

HAPPY HALLOWEEN!

There are plenty of frights in the Halloween episode, but when Max, wearing a Mike Myers mask, jumps out at the boys, it's best not to be holding the popcorn.

WILL'S TAKEOVER

When we first see the Mind Flayer's huge tentacles go into Will's eyes, nose and mouth in Season Two it's the scariest moment so far. And when Will starts screeching as they burn the tunnels it's even worse.

ELEVEN'S LEG WOUND

When a blob of the Mind Flayer gets stuck in El's leg and starts wiggling around in there, Jonathan attempts to pull it out, until El uses all her powers to suck it out. We think our stomachs turned Upside Down.

BILLY GETS FLAYED

Billy has always been a scary, aggressive character but when he gets possessed by the Mind Flayer he becomes a new level of terrifying. "I want you to build". Urgh.

STRANGER SPECULATION

SEASON 4

While we wait for Season Four let's mull over what *could* happen.

Things could get nuclear

This trailer for Season Four reveals Hopper is still alive and in Russia. One theory goes that the next season will take place around April 1986, and this is when the Chernobyl disaster occurred. Could the Russian nuclear leak end up being caused or indeed fabricated in an attempt to cover-up a battle involving Eleven, the Russians introduced in Season Three and a whole host of other creatures? What's Russian for "possibly"?

"WE ARE NOT IN HAWKINS ANYMORE"

The trailer also flashed up with these words. So maybe we'll be following Joyce and family to their new town? "[Season Four is] going to open up a little bit ... not necessarily in terms of scale, in terms of special effects, but open up in terms of allowing plotlines into areas outside of Hawkins," said Matt Duffer. "We just have to keep adjusting the story – though I don't know if we can justify something bad happening to them once a year."

WE'RE NOT IN HAWKINS ANYMORE

ELEVEN GOES BAD

The writing team of *Stranger Things* shared the lyrics to Florence and the Machine's song *Cosmic Love* as a teaser for Season Four. They are 'And in the dark, I can hear your heartbeat I tried to find the sound, But then it stopped, and I was in the darkness, so darkness I became.' Ooh cryptic. Some fans have argued that this means Eleven becomes the monster.

Suzie is the spy

Is Dustin's camp girlfriend a double agent working for the Russians? Gaten Matarazzo had this to say: "My favourite theory is that Suzie's actually a Russian mastermind and spy working with the Russian government. I think it's so stupid and so funny. I hope that doesn't play out because that would be weird."

REMEMBER NOVEMBER?

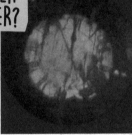

Fans have zoomed in on the trailer for Season Four and found that the clock reads 11. Is this a reference to Eleven going bad? Or does it mean that the show will come out in the 11th month? Some people have argued that a clock symbolises going back in time, and someone will rewind the clock and go back and save Hopper.

Looking into the future is a scary thing.

It might be the last

"The truth is we're definitely going four seasons and there's very much the possibility of a fifth," said *Stranger Things* producer Shawn Levy. "Beyond that, it becomes I think very unlikely."

"THE DEMOGORGON ... IT GOT ME."

WILL BYERS

The D&D fan has been through a lot, and that's just his haircut.

WILL

"Wiiiiiilll"

You've got to feel sorry for Will. Not only does he get trapped in The Upside Down and get possessed by the Mind Flayer, but in Season Three no one wants to play *Dungeons and Dragons* with him. Why can't this kid catch a break?

Will, you can cycle away from monsters, but not the bowl your mum uses to cut your hair.

He's tough

He can't flip a van with his mind or crack the jokes, but Will is the most resilient character on the show. First he survived a week alone in The Upside Down, and then he stood his ground and told the Shadow Monster to "Go away!" It didn't turn out too well, but credit where it's due.

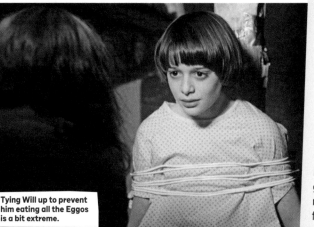

Tying Will up to prevent him eating all the Eggos is a bit extreme.

Will the Wise

Will is one of the kindest and most compassionate characters on the show. When Will is being controlled by the Mind Flayer, his friends and family try to remind him of who he really is. Joyce recalls how he once gave his toy truck to a little girl, and Mike shares the moment they become friends. Aww you guys!

Crazy together

Will's friendship with Mike is particularly touching. We see it on Halloween night, when Will doesn't know if his visions of The Upside Down are real, and Mike still misses Eleven. But Mike, ever the protector of the party, reassures Will with a smile: "Hey, well, if we're both going crazy, then we'll go crazy together, right?"

Is Will gay?

When the boys argue in Season Three, Mike says to Will, "It's not my fault you don't like girls!" In pitch notes for the show, the Duffer brothers describe Will as "a sweet, sensitive kid with sexual identity issues." Maybe this will be explored in Season Four.

MEET NOAH

NOAH SCHNAPP was only 11 when he was cast as Will Byers on *Stranger Things*, but he's been acting since he was six years old. He auditioned for the part of Mike, but the Duffer brothers called him back to play Will. He's close friends with Millie Bobbie Brown, and they post pictures of each other on Instagram. Noah says that when fans approach him, they usually say, "I found Will!". Good one, guys.

HOW BIG A STRANGER THINGS FAN ARE YOU?

Think you know Hawkins inside out and upside down? Take our challenge and find out.

1. What is Eleven's real name?
a) Sarah
b) Jane
c) El

2. How did Barb cut her hand?
a) Opening a beer
b) Making a sandwich
c) She fell over

3. Which 80s movie poster is on Jonathan's bedroom wall?
a) *The Shining*
b) *The Goonies*
c) *The Evil Dead*

4. Who dances with Max at the Winter Ball?
a) Dustin
b) Lucas
c) Will

5. What is the school bully's name in Season One?
a) Travis
b) Troy
c) Trey

6. What snack is Keith always eating?
a) Cheetos
b) Doritos
c) Apples

7. What is Max's name on the arcade games?
a) Maximilian
b) Mad Max
c) Max Factor

8. What is Kali's power?
a) Time travel
b) Create illusions
c) Flying

9. When Joyce identifies Will's body, what does she look for?
a) A scar
b) A birthmark
c) A third nipple

10. What is the name of Hopper's daughter who died?
a) Sarah
b) Katie
c) Hannah

11. Billy and Max come from ...?
a) California
b) Florida
c) Georgia

12. How much does Hopper want Eleven to leave the door open?
a) 12 inches
b) 1 inch
c) 3 inches

13. Where does the Mind Flayer take Billy?
a) Gas works
b) The bank
c) Steel works

14. Hopper's code name is 'Antique ...' what?
a) Chariot
b) Wheelbarrow
c) Motorbike

15. Which newspaper do Nancy and Jonathan work for?
a) *The Hawkins Post*
b) *The Hawkins Mail*
c) *The Hawkins Gazette*

16. Which song does Suzie ask Dustin to sing?
a) *The Neverending Story*
b) *Somewhere Over The Rainbow*
c) *Material Girl*

17. What flavour Slurpee does Alexei ask for?
a) Cherry
b) Strawberry
c) Banana

18. What is Lucas's middle name?
a) Donald
b) Philip
c) Charles

19. What book is Mrs Wheeler reading at the pool?
a) *Tender Is The Night*
b) *Tender Is The Storm*
c) *Tender Is My Heart*

20. What is the password to enter Castle Byers?
a) Radagast
b) Merlin
c) Druid

ANSWERS: 1b, 2a, 3c, 4b, 5b, 6a, 7b, 8b, 9b, 10a, 11a, 12c, 13c, 14a, 15a, 16a, 17b, 18c, 19b, 20a.

YOUR SCORE

1-7 Poops ahoy!
You need some help to ace this test (where's Barb when you need her?). What would Mr Clarke say? Go and watch more *Stranger Things* and stop getting distracted by Steve's hair.

8-13 Middle ground
You're getting there, but you found some questions harder than fighting a Demogorgon. Maybe you're just a bit sloppy like a Season One Hopper. Try harder next time if you want to save the world.

14-20 Will the Wise
You're smarter than Robin when she cracks the Russian code about the mall. You can remember more under pressure than Suzie with Planck's Constant. You would win every D&D campaign for sure. You're a SUPER FAN!

MORE
SECRETS
FROM
THE SET

You thought that was all the goss? Think again!

The Nether?

The Upside Down was referred to as "the Nether" in the original scripts and even on set during the first season's filming. But once the series aired and fans honed in on the language used when Eleven and the boys flip over the *Dungeons and Dragons* board, the term Upside Down stuck.

ALL THAT GLITTERS

Production of the show halted for a brief period of time because Millie Bobbie Brown showed up to set inexplicably covered completely in glitter. No, they never figured out where the glitter came from. No, they never have to worry about that type of thing happening to David Harbour.

Naaaancy!

British actor Charlie Heaton, who plays Jonathan Byers, had some trouble with his American accent - specifically the word Nancy. Which was awkward as he says it a lot. They ended up having to re-record Jonathan's dialogue to Americanise his Nancys.

Give me an A ...

Winona Ryder painted her Ouija board alphabet wall in one take. "We needed to get that right in one take; otherwise it would've been 45 minutes to bring in a different wall," says ST producer Shawn Levy. "So Winona was really aware that she could not screw it up. And she nailed the alphabet in a straight line without too much paint splatter or drip in one take."

Dog days

One of the show's writers was a stand-in for the Demodog. Writer Katy Trefery happened to be on set when they were filming Bob's death, and The Duffer brothers realised she was about the right size for a Demodog. They had her sit over Sean Astin and attack him like a Demodog in order to accurately CGI the monster in later.

Trick or treat

The gang are famous for being friends in real life (they even have a group chat called Stranger Texts), and they went out on Halloween together. "This one kid was like, 'Are you the cast from Stranger Things?'" MBB explained. "And I was like, 'No, I'm Harley Quinn.'"

THE REAL STARCOURT

Starcourt Mall in Season Three was a real-life shopping mall on the outskirts of Atlanta. "Everything you see in Season Three is real, which allowed for big, long continuous takes from outside to inside," says Shawn Levy. "But if you walked 50 yards in one direction, there were actual real 2019 people shopping at contemporary stores. So it was very surreal."

"HELLO LADIES ..."

STEVE HARRINGTON

STEVE

From school douchebag, to the best babysitter in town, Steve is a fan favourite.

Steve used a lot of Farrah Fawcet hairspray that day.

Holding out for a hero

Steve is always risking his life for his friends. In Season One, he comes back to the Byers house to help attack the Demogorgon with a bat. In Season Two, he fends off a pack of ravenous Demodogs and punches big bad boy Billy. In Season Three, he drives his car into Flayed Billy, saving the whole gang. As Dustin says "he's awesome!"

Chick magnet

Whether he's winking, saying "hello ladies" or climbing through Nancy's bedroom window, it's easy to see why King Steve is the heart-throb of Hawkins. And don't even get us started on that hair.

Steve and Dustin argue about who farted in the lift.

Bromance for the ages

Steve and Dustin's love for each other is strong. Favourite moments include Steve's girl advice to Dustin before the ball ("You're gonna slay 'em dead"), their secret handshakes and his reaction when Dustin comes back from summer camp. "How many children are you friends with?" asks Robin.

He steps down graciously

When Nancy chooses Jonathan over Steve, he takes it on the chin. He knows he has been a bad boyfriend but "it turns out I'm a pretty damn good babysitter". Yeah you are! When he tells Robin he has feelings for her, but she likes Tammy Thompson, he's immediately accepting, and thinks Robin could do better. Good reaction, Steve.

Steve and Robin

From her teasing him about his lack of prowess with girls (the You Suck whiteboard), to Steve telling Dustin how great Robin is ("She's so funny, she's hilarious") the bond between Steve and Robin is *ST* gold. Give these two their own series!

MEET JOE

JOE KEERY was born in 1992 in Massachusetts, and was acting in TV shows, adverts and films before he was cast as Steve. The cocky jock was only meant to be in one series, but the Duffer brothers loved Joe so much, they made his part bigger. Joe was in a band called Post Animal before *Stranger Things*. He says "Do I get recognised? I guess it depends on if I'm wearing a hat or not. The hairdo is a dead giveaway."

LOVED AND LOST

All the characters who didn't make it. RIP you guys!

BENNY

This kindly diner owner feeds Eleven fries, and is one of the first and most shocking deaths on the show when 'social services' aka Agent Connie comes in and shoots him.

BARB

She may have finally got a funeral in Season Two, but the moment when we realise Barb has actually died is heartbreaking for Nancy. And for us. We all loved Barb.

HEATHER

Billy's fellow lifeguard seemed like a lovely girl. Until the Mind Flayer got her and she abducted her parents. Sadly, like a lot of Hawkins residents she got melted into the Mind Flayer and died.

MEWS

Dustin's beloved cat got eaten by Dart. He may have been replaced by another cat – Tews – but we'll never forget this furry friend.

BOB

Joyce's boyfriend Bob Newby was adorable, so it was really sad when he sacrificed himself to save the rest of the gang. He reprogrammed the computers in the lab so that they could run away, but a Demodog attacked him in the process. He lives on in Season Three in Will's drawing of him as a superhero. SuperBob to the rescue!

There's always one person who takes fancy dress too far.

BILLY

He may have been a bully in life, but in death Billy sacrificed himself to the Mind Flayer to save Eleven. His final words are 'I'm sorry'. Poor Billy.

RIP TBC ...?

HOPPER

Did he? Didn't he? Watch this space.

DR BRENNER

Eleven's 'Papa' at the lab looked like he got eaten, but Season Two claimed he's still alive.

MRS DRISCOLL

This little old lady became one of the Flayed. But not before eating all the fertiliser and going all veiny in the hospital. Bad times.

ALEXEI

The Russian scientist kidnapped by Hopper and Joyce was living the dream when he was shot by Grigori at the fun fair. May your heaven be filled with strawberry Slurpees, Alexei.

WHICH STRANGER THINGS CHARACTER

AM I?

Let's open the curiosity door and find out.

1. I ask Eleven to make the *Millennium Falcon* fly. I am ...?
- a) Dustin
- b) Mike
- c) Hopper
- d) Dr Brenner

2. I like watching *He-Man and the Masters of the Universe* on TV. I am ...?
- a) Lucas
- b) Billy
- c) Max
- d) Eleven

4. I have a poster of Tom Cruise on my wall. I am ...?
- a) Mrs Wheeler
- b) Nancy
- c) Hopper
- d) Joyce

3. I took down Jonathan's poster for *The Evil Dead*. I am ...?
- a) Joyce
- b) Nancy
- c) Lonnie
- d) Will

5. I'm a photographer for the Hawkins Post. I am ...?
- a) Nancy
- b) Jonathan
- c) Joyce
- d) Bob

6. I attacked Billy at the Steel Works. I am ...?
- a) The Mind Flayer
- b) The Demogorgon
- c) Max
- d) Eleven

7. My middle name is Charles. I am ..?
a) Steve
b) Lucas
c) Mike
d) Dustin

8. I don't want to be dressed as Winston for Halloween. I am ..?
a) Lucas
b) Mike
c) Eleven
d) Will

9. I love a Strawberry Slurpee. I am ...?
a) Alexei
b) Robin
c) Erica
d) Murray

10. I had a crush on Tammy Thompson at school. I am ...?
a) Steve
b) Mike
c) Billy
d) Robin

ANSWERS

1a, 2d, 3a, 4c, 5b, 6b, 7b, 8a, 9a, 10d.

YOUR SCORE

8-10 Super Fan
Did you write *Stranger Things*? Are you one of the Duffer brothers? If not, we're very impressed. You really know your stuff!

4-7 Time for a rewatch
You know more than Will than Wise. And that's saying something. But if you want an excuse to watch more ST, we wont stop you.

1-3 Have you even seen ST?
Like Steve, you might need to be kept back a year so you get a higher score next time. That's OK, we won't make you wear a sailor outfit.

"DUMP HIS ASS."

MAX MAYFIELD

MAX

Maxine 'Mad Max' Mayfield is the queen of sass.

Don't mess with Max

Whether she calls Dustin and Lucas "the stalkers" or she's calling out Mike for not liking her, Max has some serious attitude and we like it.

Coolest character?

From the moment she skateboards into our lives from California, Max seems seriously cool. She whoops the boys' asses at arcade games, she takes on Billy with the baseball bat of nails, *and* she can drive a car.

The passing of the sacred skateboard shows these two are true friends.

Max-El moments

We love that Max and Eleven become great friends and an iconic duo. We also love that Max teaches Eleven so much, not only that there's more to life than boys, but also how to go shopping. "You keep trying things on until something feels like you".

She's tough

Max has a hard time, with her mean stepbrother Billy and Mike saying that she's annoying and she can't join the group. But she doesn't ever give up. Eleven might have powers, but Max is the powerful one.

Lu-max love

These guys might bicker all the time, but they love each other really. When Lucas tells her "you're cool, you're different, you're super smart, and you're like totally tubular", we couldn't agree more.

MEET SADIE

SADIE SINK was born in 2002 in Texas and played Annie on Broadway before winning the part of Max on *Stranger Things*. She had to wear fake tan to play California girl Max and learned to skateboard for the role. Sadie revealed it took them two days to film the mall montage scene where she takes Eleven shopping. "It was really great to let loose and not be fighting back tears or being terrified for once. You need to be silly sometimes."

STRANGEST MOMENTS

WEIRD
JUST SAYING

**That little town of Hawkins seems nice.
Oh wait a minute ...**

SEASON 1... STRANGE

Will vanishing
**The strange-o-meter, like the
show, is just getting started.**

Body of evidence
**The body they drag out the lake isn't
Will, and it's stuffed full of cotton wool.**

Telekinetic powers
**Eleven can crush coke cans, stop
noisy fans, flip vans and open and
shut the gate to The Upside Down.
"She's basically a wizard" as Dustin
puts it.**

Exploding phones
**Poor Joyce is on her third phone
by only the second episode.**

R-I-G-H-T-H-E-R-E
**Will can communicate through
Christmas lights, and monsters can pop
out of the wall. No big deal.**

SEASON 2 ... STRANGER

008
Kali can make people see things that aren't there.

Tadpoles
When kids have pets in Hawkins, their faces open up and they eat cats.

SEASON 3 ... STRANGEST

Melting rats
Lots and lots of them. Which slither off somewhere. Urgh.

Melting people
The possessed citizens of Hawkins melt together to form a giant human flesh monster. Nice.

HONOURABLE MENTIONS

Although the main characters get all the glory, these guys have a special place in our hearts.

TED WHEELER

Nancy and Mike's dad only cares about three things – his La-Z-boy chair, his lawn and where he left his glasses. We love how little he notices anything going on. No wonder Karen had her head turned by Billy at the pool. Zzzz.

MR CLARKE

The gang's teacher knows everything and helps them save the world. Often without realising it.

MRS HENDERSON

We want Dustin's mum to be our mum. When she asks him "Are you constipated again?" she became our favourite parent.

KEITH

This super geek runs the arcade and then the video shop, he loves Nancy and Cheetos. And we love him.

DR SAM OWENS

We were never sure whether to trust him or not, but we think he's on the right team. He sticks up for Will and helps Hopper adopt Eleven.

KALI

Eleven's sister 008 didn't get to do much, but we'd love to see more of her in future seasons. And to discover some other number kids too!

MURRAY BAUMAN

Sarcastic, smart and super paranoid. Who could forget how much we love this 'freelance journalist' in hiding?

MAYOR KLINE

The sleazy corrupt mayor of Hawkins deserved every punch he had coming to him from Hopper. But we love to hate a good baddie.

"I BREAK THINGS."

BILLY HARGROVE

Max's stepbrother is the ultimate bad boy who comes good in the end.

BILLY

"That's how you do it, Hawkins"

Billy arrived on the scene with his stepsister Max and instantly made an impression. He was drinking beer from a keg upside down, beating Steve at basketball and spending a lot of time with his shirt off.

Billy, never knowingly not topless.

He's got issues

OK, so Billy might be mean (he's horrible to Max and nearly runs over her friends) but we find out why when we meet his abusive dad. Like many bullies, Billy's been bullied himself. It's just that now he's taking it out on Max and her crew. In Season Three we learn about his tragic past. No wonder he's so messed up.

Is it hot in here?

With his mullet, earring and cheesy chat up lines (he tells Mrs Wheeler "I didn't realise Nancy had a sister"), Billy is the hunkiest lifeguard in Hawkins. And doesn't he know it.

Should I flay or should I go?

When he gets possessed by the Mind Flayer, Billy tries his best to fight him off. He tells Mrs Wheeler to leave him alone instead of hurting her, but eventually the Flaying overpowers him and he attacks Heather.

But just when all seemed lost ...

Eleven manages to get through to Billy by talking about his memories, and he makes the ultimate sacrifice – stopping the Mind Flayer from getting El. His last words are 'I'm sorry' to Max. Bye Billy.

MEET DACRE

DACRE MONTGOMERY was born in Perth, Australia in 1994. He got the role of Billy after performing his audition tape in underwear and sunglasses doing a dance to 80s music. "Billy is an unpredictable character. I think there were two outcomes: I was never going to work in this industry again, or somebody somewhere was going to see something in me." Luckily it was the latter.

MOST ROMANTIC MOMENTS

Love is in the air in Hawkins ... here are the cutest couples.

When Lucas opens up to Max in the arcade and tells her the truth about what happened the year before, he makes himself vulnerable to her. She returns the favour on top of the junkyard bus, telling him about her difficult home life. We also love it when he breaks her out of her bedroom on his bike. Aww, you guys!

LUCAS + MAX

They share their first kiss at school at the end of Season One. By Season Three they're having make-out sessions in Eleven's room (much to Hopper's dismay). But the moment when Mike admits he loves Eleven, and she later says it back to him, is too cute for words.

ELEVEN + MIKE

That spark between them exploded when they spent the night together at Murray Bauman's. After everything they'd been through together and how their relationship had grown, it was satisfying to see them make their romance official. Will they be able to maintain a long-distance love now that Jonathan and his family have left Hawkins?

NANCY + JONATHAN

Whether they're making out in the stationery cupboard or dancing together on Halloween night, Bob is the knight in shining armour Joyce has been waiting for (after Will and Jonathan's dad Lonny was so useless in Season One). But sadly Joyce and Bob's time together is short, making their moments together all the more poignant.

JOYCE + BOB

Over a shared cigarette at Joyce's kitchen table we discovered that these two go waaay back. He helped her find her son, and bring him home, and she returns the favour when he's stuck in The Upside Down. We realise he's jealous of her new relationship when he asks "How's Bob the Brain?" They hold hands at the fairground and decide to go on a real date. Alas, it's not to be.

JOYCE + HOPPER

"HEY DINGUS!"

ROBIN BUCKLEY

ROBIN

Steve's Scoops Ahoy sidekick became one of our all-time favourite characters.

Robin = Genius

Of course it's Robin Buckley who translates the secret Russian spy code during a single shift at Scoops Ahoy. She's fluent in four languages! She also came up with the strategy of getting the blueprints of the mall to find the air ducts. This girl is like Einstein if he happened to have a summer job in an ice-cream parlour.

She's funny

Robin gets some of the best, most sarcastic lines on the show. When Steve tells her he can read she says "Since when?"

Even death doesn't scare her

Robin spits in the scary Russian man's face. She laughs in the face of death (quite literally when her and Steve get drugged). And as she tells Dustin "We all die my strange little child friend, it's just a matter of how and when".

Can we be friends?

We'd love to be friends with Robin. She tends to Steve when he gets hurt by the Russians. She explains the plot of *Back to the Future* to him. And she gets him a job in a video store. How do we make her our friend?

Bathroom moment

When Robin comes out to Steve in the toilet stall it's a big sensitive, emotional moment for the show. Poor Steve doesn't get it "But Tammy Thompson's a girl?!" Yes, Steve, catch up!

MEET MAYA

MAYA HAWKE is the daughter of actors Uma Thurman and Ethan Hawke. She was born in 1998 and played Jo March in the BBC adaptation of *Little Women*. Hawke revealed that she and the Duffers didn't decide that Robin should be a lesbian until they were around halfway through filming the season. "It was kind of a collaborative conversation, and I'm really, really happy with the way that it went," she said.

GOOD HAIR DAY

Hawkins' best hair styles.

Eleven's hair raising changes

From her iconic buzzcut in Season One, Eleven progresses to wild unkempt curls and then a slicked back punk look, and finally a wavy bob in Season Three, which mirrors new BFF Max's tousled locks. Accessorised with a big yellow scrunchie, obvs.

Steve 'the hair' Harrington

Steve is known for his luscious locks, and in Season Two we find out exactly how he gets them so perfect. Faberge Organics shampoo and conditioner, four spritzes of Farrah Fawcett hairspray while damp, and voilà! A majestic mullet. We're taking a picture of "The Steve" into the hairdresser next time.

Will's bowl cut

Noah Schnapps had to wear hair extensions to create Will's dorky haircut. One which everyone has had at some point when they were younger. Get the bowl out, Mum!

Dustin's 'do

When Dustin takes Steve's advice and gets ready for the Snow Ball, he ends up with a towering curly mullet which looks a bit like he's stuck his fingers in a plug socket.

Billy's crowning glory

Giving Steve a run for his money in the grooming department, Billy's tousled blond mane is quite something. Dacre Montgomery has revealed it's actually a wig.

Nancy's perm power

We love how Nancy's hair gets bigger as her character gains in confidence. Her tight corkscrew curls were so 80s, but our favourite hairstyle is in Season Three. You can tell she's a serious journalist because of her serious 'do. Apparently, the show's hairstylist used Winona Ryder's old wig to make Natalia's bouncy bouffant.

"JUST THE FACTS."

ERICA SINCLAIR

Lucas' snarky little sister steals the show in Season Three.

ERICA

"Nerd"

Erica's main purpose in life is to publicly bring her brother down a peg or two. When Lucas is having his photo taken on Halloween, she's all "God, you are such a nerd. No wonder you only hang out with boys." After being told off, Erica is momentarily silenced, but not even that can keep her from mouthing an accusatory "nerd" at her brother. With little sisters like this, who needs enemies?

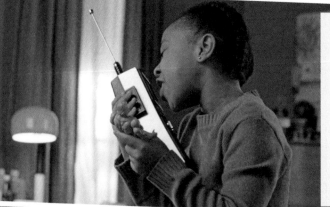

She's a mini sass machine

Erica is always annoyed with Lucas, and with his friends. So when Dustin is screaming into a walkie talkie in Season Two, she answers his call. "Could you please shut up? Code red? I got a code for you instead. It's called code shut your mouth." Ooh salty.

Erica for president

When Dustin tries to guilt Erica into taking part in the scheme - a scheme that Erica herself refers to as Operation Child Endangerment – she comes up with one of her best lines. As part of his attempt, Dustin asks Erica if she's a patriot who loves her country - to which Erica offers the absolutely perfect reply, "you can't spell America without Erica." You can't have *Stranger Things* without her either.

Free. Ice-cream. For. Life!

After she listens to Dustin, Steve and Robin's plans for her to crawl through the air ducts in the Starcourt Mall, she makes sure she gets something out of the deal. In exchange for her services, Erica has a simple request: she wants free ice cream from Scoops Ahoy, whenever she asks for it. No doubt she found a way to claim this, despite the mall having burned down.

No one is safe

Steve, Robin and Dustin are "So nerdy you make me physically ill". When Lucas says "Isn't it past your bedtime?" She fires back "Isn't it time you died?" But, y'know, just the facts.

MEET PRIAH

PRIAH FERGUSON was born in Atlanta, Georgia – where the show is filmed – in 2006. She was only meant to have a small part, but she impressed the Duffers so much, they made Erica a big role in Season Three. To prepare, Priah did her research. "I listened to 80s music like *Computer Love* and I would watch movies like *E.T.*," she says. Note that Lucas' sister inherits the boys' *Dungeons and Dragons* manual at the end of Season Three - Erica spin-off here we come!

TOP 10 QUOTES

Our favourite ever *ST* quotes.
Try and use one in a sentence today.

1. "SHE'S OUR FRIEND AND SHE'S CRAZY!"

When Dustin screams this about Eleven it's a very bonding moment for the whole gang. Everyone has one friend they could shout this about. You're thinking about them right now.

3. "DID YOU HEAR THE ONE ABOUT THE FAT MAN WITH THE BEARD WHO CLIMBS DOWN CHIMNEYS?"

Hopper says this in response to Murray's conspiracy theories (while spitting out an apple), but it's a great line to say to anyone who's saying something silly and unbelievable.

4. "ARE YOU TRYING TO ASK ME TO DANCE STALKER?"

Max says this to Lucas, pretending she doesn't already love him. We can really picture saying this to our crush.

5. "I'M STEALTHY, LIKE A NINJA."

Steve Harrington thinks he's got all the ninja skills but we reckon we do, too. We like to say this after stealing another biscuit and getting away with it.

2. "MY EARS ARE LITTLE GENIUSES."

OK, so we haven't cracked a Russian code like Robin, but we like to think we're good listeners.

6. "FRIENDS DON'T LIE."

Eleven got this off Mike and not a truer word was ever spoken. Honesty is everything. Especially when you're saving the world.

7. "NOBODY NORMAL EVER ACCOMPLISHED ANYTHING MEANINGFUL IN THE WORLD."

Jonathan has this so right. Weirdos of the world unite.

8. "KEEP SAYING MY NAME, SEE WHAT HAPPENS."

Sassy-mouthed Erica has so many quotable lines, but this is one we just love to deliver. Preferably with a hair toss.

9. "ASK FOR FORGIVENESS, NOT PERMISSION."

This is a Nancy-ism and we're totally trying it next time we want to get away with something.

10. "IF YOU BELIEVE IN THIS STORY ... FINISH IT."

We loved it when Mrs Wheeler gave Nancy a kitchen pep talk. Although it applies to her article, we think it applies to many things in life. Mrs Wheeler knows a thing or two.

STRANGER THINGS
LEXICON

ARE YOU FLUENT?

This 80s slang is totally bitchin'.

BITCHIN' *(noun)*
Very good.
"Bitchin." – Eleven

CHILL *(verb, adjective)*
To relax or be calm.
As in "We can just, just like, chill in my car ..." – Steve or "I'm chill." – Barb

DINGUS *(noun)*
A loveable idiot.
"That was Pig Latin, dingus." – Robin.

DOUCHEBAG *(noun)*
An obnoxious or contemptible person.
As in "You're such a douchebag, Mike!" – Nancy, or "It's because she's been dating that douchebag, Steve Harrington." – Lucas.

KNUCKLEHEAD *(noun)*
A stupid person.
"Yeah, you know ... A dumb person. A knucklehead." – Mike

MOUTH BREATHER *(noun)*
A stupid person.
As in "I was tripped by this mouth breather Troy, OK?" – Mike

SLING *(verb)*
To sell.
"In the meantime sling ice cream, behave and don't get beat up." – Robin.

TUBULAR *(noun)*
Awesome or excellent.
As in "You're like totally tubular." – Lucas

WASTOID *(noun)*
A waste of space.
As in "I just, didn't want you to think I was such a wastoid, you know?" – Mike

WEIRDO *(noun)*
Eccentric, weird or crazy.
As in "We forget the weirdo and go straight to the gate." – Lucas

DO YOU SPEAK DUSTIN?

"NASTY-ASS RASH"
(acne)

"MENTAL"
(crazy)

"CURIOSITY PADDLES"
(books)

"LANDO!"

Dustin uses the word Lando as shorthand for Lando Calrissian from *Star Wars*. He invited Darth Vader to dinner and lead Han Solo and friends into a trap. Next time you feel like someone has double-crossed or betrayed you for their own gain (noble or otherwise), be sure to yell 'LANDO!'

ELEVEN-ISMS

Eleven only says 246 words in Season One of *Stranger Things* ... most of them are:

"PAPA"

"BAD PLACE"

"NO!"

"PRETTY"

CREDITS

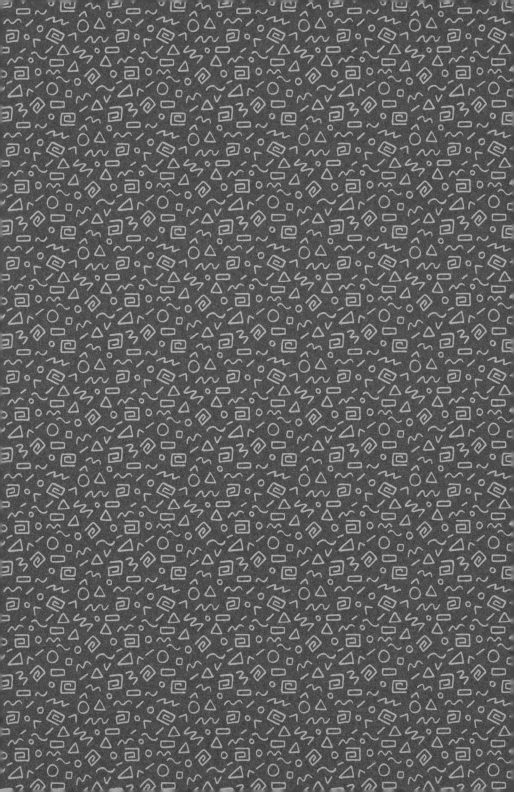

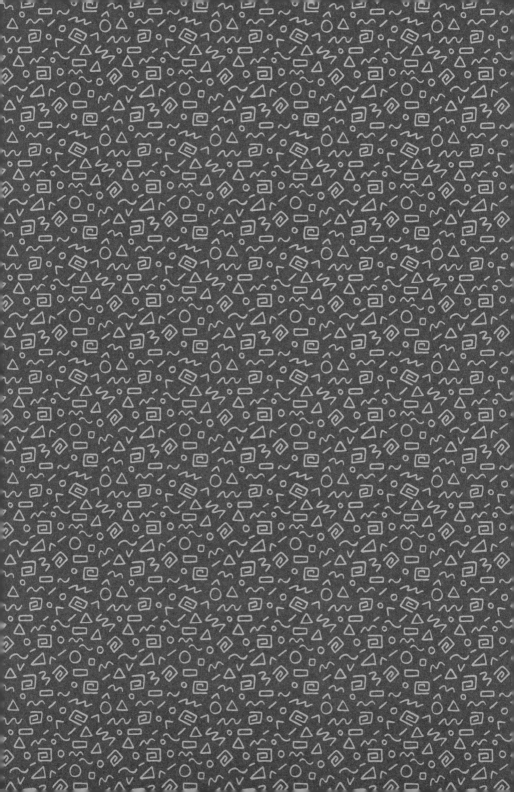